The Secret Pink Rose

Niharika Chopra

INVINCIBLE PUBLISHERS

First published in India in 2017 by Invincible Publishers

ISBN: 978-93-86148-99-5

Invincible Publishers
G-120, Sushant Lok III, Sector 57,
Gurgaon-122002

Digitally Printed at Replika Press Pvt. Ltd.

For my younger sister ***Dhruvi,*** *who is waiting for the Princess of the story to find her Prince Charming,*

For ***Ishika,*** *who questioned every move of the princess inquisitively,*

For ***Yuvaansh,*** *for having the patience to wait till the book was published.*

Acknowledgement

I thank God for clearing all hurdles out of my way to accomplish my first piece of writing. I am grateful to my wonderful family and friends for their unfaltering support and inspiration.

I owe special gratitude to my mother and maasi for their constant motivation and support.

I am grateful to Invincible Publishers for converting my story into a book.

Table of Contents

Introduction

Once upon a time, there was a beautiful young princess named Rosepink. She was named after a charming pink rose, which was believed to be *magical*.

Old people of the kingdom were sure that one day something magical will happen with princess Rosepink, but nothing like that had ever happened.

Rosepink was named by her mother, Queen Lusida. Her mother had a big garden near her castle, which was full of different and beautiful flowers. One of them was the *pink rose plant* that kept blooming throughout the year. Be it autumn or spring, the rose always kept flowering. She liked that pink rose very much; in fact, it was her favorite flower. She named her daughter after the pink rose. She wanted her daughter to bloom forever just like the rose and remain healthy and calm, whatever the situation be.

Rosepink lost her dear mother, Queen Lusida when she was just two years old. Despite her mother dying so early, her father looked after her very well. Her father always loved her and tried to keep her happy so that she never felt the absence of her mother in her life.

Rosepink was kind, caring, and simple and everyone loved her. When she was about eight and a half years old, something magical happened with her.

Where did my necklace go?
Let me look among the flowers!

The Lost Necklace

Rosepink used to go for a walk in her garden daily and loved to climb up the trees. She used to pluck fruits with the help of her friends and then they all used to make marmalades, shakes etc. out of them. She liked to sit in front of the buttercup river in her garden (a spot full of buttercup flowers). Behind this spot was the pink rose surrounded by many colorful and beautiful rose bushes but the pink rose stood out brightly and attracted everyone.

This was the same rose, which her mother liked a lot. One day, Rosepink was roaming in her garden, where she slipped and her precious necklace (which was gifted to her by her beloved mom), fell and landed on the petals of the pink rose. When she kneeled down to pick it up, suddenly it vanished.

She was astonished to see this, as there was no one else near that rose! Then how did her precious necklace disappear?

Rosepink was an adventurous and curious girl so she didn't go back to the castle to inform her father about what had happened. She was determined that she would go and look for it by herself, without taking anybody's help.

As Rosepink was thinking what to do next, she noticed that a pretty pink butterfly sat on the rose and then magically it entered inside the rose. By now, she was sure that the pink rose is magical. "But what kind of magic is there in this pink rose?" she thought to herself.

Rosepink started looking very carefully at and around the pink rose. While trying to peep inside the rose, she lost her balance and fell upon it. Everything happened so quickly that she was not able to understand that what was going on. Actually, she was drawn into the flower by magical powers. While being pulled inside, she fainted.

When Rosepink regained consciousness, she saw a cramped dirty place with dry leaves all over the ground. After wandering a little, she caught sight of a staircase. The steps were steep. It looked like a very old staircase, full of soil and broken pieces of thin wood that seemed to be parts of very old and dried roots. It was a narrow staircase with walls on both sides. She then saw roots of a plant coming out of these walls. The staircase made crackling sounds as she descended. On her way down, she was pleasantly surprised to find her precious necklace. She picked up the necklace, wiped it with her gown and wore it again. Being an inquisitive girl, she stepped down the rest of stairs to see what that place actually was.

When she reached bottom of the stairs, she saw nothing but an old wooden door. The door too was full of dust and had spider webs. She hesitatingly opened the door and saw a bench, a small wooden table on which a jug full of lemonade and some empty cups.

To her surprise, the bench was clean and well maintained. The lemonade also looked fresh. It seemed as if someone had just cleaned the room.

She looked around. The room was small and had walls of wood. There was sunlight falling in the room through the cracks in the wood.

It was a perfect place to take rest for a while. She was very tired so she had the lemonade and rested for some time.

She got up and tried to peep out of the cracks in the wooden wall. All she could see was bright daylight. She tried to stretch the crack a little bit with her hands. To her surprise, the wall moved to one side like a sliding door. She saw another flight of stairs behind that door. The opening was too small for her to pass. She bent and squeezed herself a bit to pass through it. She then descended the stairs that led her to another small room.

This room was even better than the previous one. It had a cupboard with some clothes that were very tiny. It had a washroom as well.

"How can such dirty, soil filled place have such mysteriously beautiful rooms?" Rosepink thought to herself and continued to look around.

The walls were yellow and had strange drawings on them. On one side were pictures of her castle, on the other side, there was a painting of the pink rose, followed by a drawing of the staircases. The room where Rosepink was sitting was also there in another painting with a couple of dwarfs sitting on the bed.

Rosepink thought that these pictures depicted how she had spent her day. She was very astonished and anxious to see it.

It was dusk by that time and she was too tired and uneasy. She was so lost in her thoughts about the secret behind the paintings that she didn't realize when she fell asleep.

WELCOME TO
DWARF WORLD

The Mystery Begins

Rosepink felt a tickle on her nose and woke up with a jerk. There was a butterfly sitting on her nose. "Oh, this looks like the same pink butterfly but how come it is so bright?" she thought.

"Oh My God! I slept here in the flower?" she said out loudly. She looked around once again and those paintings on the wall caught her attention. All the paintings were the same but not the last one. The last painting now showed Rosepink sitting on the bed instead of those dwarfs. "How is this possible? I need to find this out!" She said loudly. Then she found some food on the shelf. She had a hamburger and packed the rest of the food for herself. She stepped out of the room and found a big banner that said-

"Welcome to the Dwarf World!

The Lemonade and food served to you was Gismo's special meal.

You are now a Dwarf and Slave of Lord Gismo!"

"This is scary," Rosepink said to herself. Then she looked at herself and thought, "Oh! Why am I afraid? I am not a dwarf. This is a cool prank! But there is definitely someone behind this prank. I need to find this out. Hmmm..." She felt determined.

But, at the same time, she got upset thinking that her father would be worried about her safety and must be looking for her by now.

"Anyway, I am safe! My father knows that I am able to defend myself. So, I can spend some more time investigating this fascinating place."

She was in two minds - to stay there or return to her palace. Something within her persuaded her to stay and find out what is in store for her.

After pondering over this, she moved ahead and saw beautiful flowers, butterflies and humming bees. But, all those flowers, butterflies and bees were very small and too shiny. There was a lake on one side, which was as sparkling as a river of diamonds. The grass too was tiny and glossy. She noticed a herd of tiny deer. Some of the deer were grazing and others were drinking water from the lake. All those deer were very glittery in appearance.

"Everything is so beautiful and mysterious here," thought Rosepink.

"Wait a minute Rosy, why did you not notice this before?" she said loudly to herself, "Where are the people of this place?"

This made her feel lonely and she missed her father and friends. She wasn't scared but wanted to see them once and then come back and explore more.

Rosepink finally turned around to go back to her father. But to her horror, everything she had seen on her way, disappeared. All these events started disturbing her a lot.

The Dwarf Friends

"How will I go back home? And where are the people of this place?" she thought to herself.

She was scared but remembered what her father had taught her. "Always keep calm. Never panic. Whenever you are in a problem, take a deep breath. There is a solution to every problem."

She smiled and took a deep breath and thought calmly for some time. She decided that firstly, she will find the people of this place, and when she can do so, they can help her to go back.

So, she started looking around for

clues that could lead her somewhere. She noticed tiny little footprints, which seemed to be left by some children. She was delighted and followed the footprints. The trail of footprints disappeared abruptly in front of a small hillock. All of a sudden, she realized that she had walked a long distance and was exhausted. She sat on a stone of the hillock. Instantly, the earth started shaking and there was lightening followed by darkness. Rosepink rushed forward but she could see nothing as it had become pitch dark. She was scared but tried to keep calm.

She heard some footsteps, and saw a shadow coming towards her. Slowly the darkness wiped out and Rosepink saw a girl holding a candle.

The girl was wearing a dress made out of dried pink petals. She had curly, long and uncombed hair, which were very dirty. Rosepink was happy that she had found someone in that lonely place.

Although she was too nervous, yet

she was curious at the same time. She wanted to know that, why was the girl so shabby, and why was she so short?

"Does this mean that *Welcome to Dwarf World* banner I saw earlier is actually true? Am I really in a dwarf world?" she thought.

Rosepink gathered courage and said, "Hello! Who are you?"

The girl looked equally confused and scared and asked in reply, "Who are you?"

Rosepink sensed that the dwarf girl was confused too. So, she stepped ahead and said to the girl "I am Rosepink. Don't worry I will not harm you."

The little girl replied reluctantly, "Hi! I am Arila."

"Nice to meet you Arila!" said Rosepink.

"Follow me," she said to Rosepink and took her into a tunnel.

They both sat down, Arila served

water to Rosepink. Rosepink said, "Can I ask you a question?"

"Of course, you can!" replied another girl, who also looked like Arila.

"Who is this girl?" asked Rosepink.

The other girl replied confidently, "Hello! I am Timsi. I am…"

"Where is Nelisa?" interrupted Arila as if she did not want Timsi to interact with Rosepink.

Just then, a girl looking like Timsi and Arila, came there holding a 'Leaf' in her hand. Something was scribbled on that leaf.

"Is she Nelisa?" asked Rosepink.

"Yes! I am Nelisa," said the girl.

"Who is this girl?" asked Nelisa.

"We don't know much Nelisa. It would be better if you ask because it is you, who has the list. Not we!" answered Arila.

"Yes, I agree with Arila," added

Timsi.

"So, I hope you know what I am going to ask you," said Nelisa.

Rosepink still trying to figure out the gravity of their conversation replied in a cordial manner, "Hi Nelisa, I am Rosepink."

"Rosepink is a very different name. Who gave you this name?" asked Nelisa sternly.

"My mother, the Queen of 'Lonario'," replied Rosepink.

"In fact, I was named after this very pink rose that I am now lost in. This was her favorite flower," she added.

"Does her name match the list?" whispered Timsi.

"Have patience Timsi!" said Arila.

"It does match," hushed Nelisa.

"So can I ask you something," said Rosepink.

"Would you please wait a minute

Rosy Posy," said Timsi in a naughty and cheerful way.

"Yes, sure!" said Rosepink, smiling at Timsi.

The way, in which Rosepink was being interrogated, she sensed that the girls already knew something mysterious about her and were waiting for her.

This is the only memory of my mother I have!
Do you have any ornaments with you?

The Hidden Truth

"Rosepink, do you have any ornaments with you?" asked Nelisa.

"Yes, I have a necklace and a pair of earrings."

"Would you please show them to me? I want to see only your necklace."

"Of course!"

Nelisa then checked her necklace. "Does it match the List?" whispered Timsi again.

"Wait, let her check, Timsi," argued Arila.

Nelisa sprinkled some water on Rosepink's necklace and the face of

Rosepink's mother appeared on the pendant.

"Fabulous!" said Arila.

"Is she the one we are waiting for?" asked Timsi hopefully.

Her eyes shined brightly as she asked this.

"I think so!" replied Nelisa.

"Rosepink, before you ask us something, I want to know, do you have any magical powers?" asked Nelisa.

"Magical powers and me? No, I don't have any magical powers," replied Rosepink.

"Are you sure? You don't need to hide anything from us."

"Yes! Nelisa, I am sure."

"OK, so would you please tell us something about your family?" asked Arila.

"No, first you people tell me something about yourselves," argued

Rosepink.

"Look Rosy, you are a stranger to all of us. We would like to know about you so that we can trust you. So, you tell us about your family first," Timsi insisted.

Nelisa and Arila exchanged smiling looks in appreciation of Timsi's logic.

"I am the princess of Lonario. My mother died when I was just two years old," said Rosepink.

"How did she die?" interrupted Nelisa.

"One day she had gone for a walk with the royal maids, but did not return. We all assumed that she might have gone too deep into the forest and some wild animals might have killed her and the maids for prey.

My father looks after me. He's very loving and caring. I have everything but I still miss my mother. Oh! I miss her so much," said Rosepink sadly.

"That's it?" asked Timsi, disappointed.

"Actually, there is more," replied Rosepink.

"Hurray!" said Timsi, excitedly.

"You know, the necklace you just inspected was actually given to me by my mother. That's the only memory of my mother I have. I always keep it close to me."

"I was too young when my mother died, so I don't remember anything. My father always tells me stories of my mother – how beautiful she looked, how caring and brave she was and about how she died," said Rosepink.

"Now it is your turn guys!" she exclaimed clearing her throat.

"I think we can trust her," said Arila to Nelisa.

"I always thought so!" added Timsi.

"You all are right we can trust her," said Nelisa.

She continued, "We are the maids

of the queen of Lonario."

Rosepink was utterly thunderstruck. She looked at all three of them with her eyes wide open and was full of questions. She just couldn't believe what she had heard. It took a moment for Rosepink to accept this statement.

"I know you are astounded, but yes, we are your mother's maids. And yes, we are very much alive," Nelisa continued explaining, "Her heart was so pure and so full of love that she treated us as her friends. Then one day, I gave birth to a girl named Timsi. Your mother used to play with Timsi for hours.

After around a month, the queen gave birth to you. We all played with you. You and Timsi loved each other's company and were very fond of each other."

As she said this, Rosepink and Timsi looked affectionately at each other and smiled.

"Our life was full of happiness until one day, when your mother, some more royal maids and we went for a walk in the garden.

The queen slipped and fell near the pink rose.

She was injured a bit, so we all went to help her get up and suddenly all of us including the queen were pulled magically into this rose. We were so exhausted when we got pulled in the rose, that when we reached the room inside the rose, we could not stop ourselves from eating and drinking the available sandwiches and lemonade.

All of us were immediately reduced in height and we all became Dwarfs," she said sadly.

Wicked Gismo

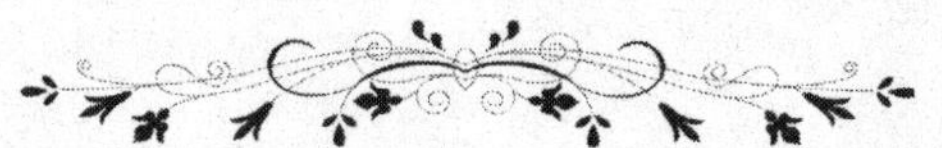

"All this was done by a witch named Gismo," Nelisa continued, "She is a very old and bad witch who wants to rule the world.

A powerful magician had trapped her inside this rose to save people of his kingdom from her wickedness.

However, she did not sit quietly in the rose. After so many years of conspiring, she was able to cast a spell that could create a kingdom of her own inside the rose itself. Now she needed people for her kingdom. She performed a magic trick with which she could pull people into the rose. Her mystical drinks shortened the height of people who were above the age of six. Timsi was two years old when she was sucked into the flower and grew for some time but stopped growing in height after she turned six."

"Rosy, were you not tired when you fell in the rose? Did you not drink that lemonade?" asked Timsi.

Before Rosepink could say anything, Nelisa explained that since Rosepink had the necklace given by her mother, she was safe.

Arila added that she remembered when they had shrunk in height, the queen had said –"Oh! If only I had my magical necklace! No magic could have ever affected me! And we could all be safe."

"But we are all Gismo's slaves now. I know you want to ask about your mom, Gismo has trapped her. We are all working for Gismo to keep our Queen and her baby princess alive."

"What do you mean by baby princess?"

"Your younger sister Rosy."

"What? Why didn't you tell me earlier Nelisa? Do you know the way to rescue them? Where are they trapped? What happened?" asked Rosepink anxiously.

"We all thought of a way to get out of this spell and tried to call the magician who had trapped Gismo in this rose.

The queen had used her magical ring and contacted the magician.

The magician appeared and listened to us. He said that he is very old now, whereas Gismo has grown powerful with time. So, he can't do anything to help us. But yes! He gave us this list and told that any girl who possesses all the qualities and things mentioned in the list can rescue us all. Moreover, if by any chance, the queen gets her magical ring and the necklace together, she could herself defeat Gismo. The 'Ring' helps the queen to perform magic and the 'Necklace' helps to save her from magic spells casted by others. Therefore, she would need both together.

The magician also told us that the only way to kill Gismo is to kill her favorite black horse. Gismo came to know of magician visiting us when the queen showed us the list. She suddenly came and snatched the ring from our beloved queen. She then took the queen and imprisoned her in a secret place. We all were made slaves and were made to work for her.

A couple of months later, we came to know through other slaves, who worked as cooks of Gismo, that the queen had given birth to a beautiful princess."

Hearing the complete story from Nelisa, Rosepink had tears in her eyes. She did not know what to do to save her mother and was eager to meet her younger sister and mother. Timsi, Nelisa and Arila were all quiet for a while so that Rosepink could recover from the shock. She was very hurt and anxious.

"Rosepink, you match this list. You have not decreased in height, you are named after this very pink rose, and you have your mother's necklace. However, you don't have any powers. You can't rescue your mother without magical powers," Nelisa said.

"Come on friends, let's just think! I am sure our Rosepink does have some powers," said Timsi.

The Warrior Princess

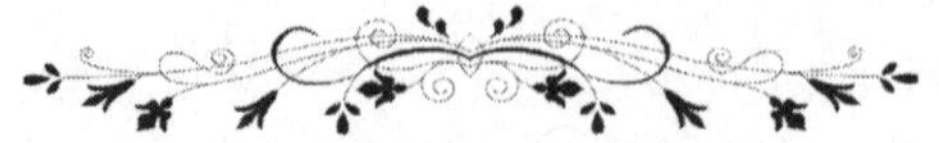

They all sat silently, trying to think deeply. All of a sudden, Timsi broke the silence by asking, "Is there any water left?"

"What do you mean?" asked Rosepink.

"The water we served was also stolen from Gismo's magical lake. We have to stitch new clothes for Gismo to earn food and water for our daily needs. These clothes are to be of new designs every time and need to be made out of dried flowers. Since this world is magical, the flowers never dry. We must work hard to pluck them and then put them into the soil so that they dry out, only then can we make dresses. When we are not able to stitch new dresses for Gismo, we go without food and water. Since a few days, we have not been able to think of new designs for her dress, so we had to steal this water to deal with our thirst. In fact, every slave here has to earn water and food through completing different tasks assigned by Gismo," told Arila.

"We don't know. You need to check, Timsi," interrupted Nelisa.

She did not want Rosepink to know about the hardships that they had to face and feel miserable.

Timsi went to check. As she was checking, a scorpion approached towards her.

Rosepink noticed everything. She knew what to do next. She picked up a sharp stone, lying near her feet and threw it towards the scorpion. It was aimed so well that the sharp edge of the stone hit the scorpion. It got killed and Timsi was safe.

Nelisa witnessed this and exclaimed

"Perfect!"

"What happened?" asked Arila.

Nelisa told her about all that had happened. "There is no water left guys," said Timsi disappointedly.

Nelisa and Arila were too occupied with their thoughts that they completely ignored Timsi's comments.

"Rosepink you aimed at the scorpion like a professional. Are you a warrior?" Nelisa's eyes lit up with hope as she asked this.

"Of course, I am! After my mother disappeared my father taught me all the warrior skills so that I could defend myself on my own," replied Rosepink.

"Fabulous!" said Nelisa and Arila in chorus.

"I am feeling very thirsty. I want water. Baaaah baaah," said Timsi in a sobbing voice.

"Relax Timsi, relax!" consoled Nelisa.

Suddenly they heard a noise. Nelisa asked Rosepink quickly to hide behind a huge rock.

Gismo's soldiers made an announcement.

"Queen is giving free water to everyone. You cannot take more than one pot."

"Let's do one thing! Rosepink, you stay hiding here! We three will go and get a pot of water each," stated Nelisa.

They came back after fifteen minutes and called out Rosepink.

"Rosy, you can sleep with Timsi. Tomorrow we will meet more people and plan out how to rescue your mother and sister," said Nelisa.

Next day, Nelisa woke up everyone early. They did not have any food left, so they had to skip breakfast. Nelisa took all of them to meet some of the other people she knew.

Timsi and Rosepink kept away while the others were talking about

Rosepink and the plan.

Nelisa then introduced Rosepink to the people there. They were very happy to see Rosepink and to know about her warrior skills. They gave her arrows and bows and a big sharp knife.

"You are now prepared to rescue some of our people," said Nelisa.

"But what is the plan?" asked Rosepink.

They explained the plan to her.

Rosepink On A Rescue Mission

They went to the castle that very night.

All of them disguised themselves in black clothes. According to the plan, Rosepink climbed up the wall and threw a rope for others. They all reached the top of the castle.

There were soldiers guarding the palace. Rosepink shot a poisonous gas arrow towards them and they all fainted.

Cautiously, they moved ahead and reached the prison. A soldier was sitting on a rock with the keys of the prison tied to a cloth on his waist. Rosepink hit the soldier on the back of his neck with her hand. He fainted and fell on the floor.

She then rescued everyone who was trapped in the prison. While going back, Rosepink shot another arrow towards the fainted soldiers and they regained consciousness.

Nobody came to know that the castle had been attacked. The soldier who was hit by Rosepink did not tell anything to Gismo fearing that she would kill him for not performing his duty carefully.

Gismo thought that the prisoners had escaped the jail and directed soldiers to catch them. Gismo was very surprised as well as furious. She could not digest that the prisoners could break away even under such strict supervision of security guards. She increased the security at other prisons and began torturing everyone even more.

Meanwhile, Nelisa and Arila took Rosepink and the rescued prisoners to a new place.

The place was exactly behind the tunnel where Rosepink had met the royal maids. Arila moved a big rock with the help of the rescued prisoners. Under that rock, there was a small cave. All the prisoners were asked to enter the cave, which was covered with muddy dried roots.

Arila instructed them to stay hidden inside, as Gismo would be looking for them. She then left to arrange for supply of food and water for them.

Next day, there was another meeting. It was decided that they should not attack two days consecutively. Thus, curious Rosepink got a little chance to investigate more about the details of the Rose world. She asked Nelisa, "How many people in total are trapped inside the rose?"

"Total seventeen from the palace. Also, we have some more people here, who are good warriors. We trained them as much as we could. When they attacked Gismo, they tried their best, but were defeated. Now Gismo has imprisoned them too and does not give them any food or water. They have become so weak that they cannot even stand properly leave alone fighting."

"We are twenty-five people if you include them."

"Tomorrow's mission is to rescue them all Rosy," said Arila.

"The people I rescued yesterday seem different. I mean I don't think that they are my mother's maids."

"You are right. They are the people Gismo had imprisoned before she trapped us," said Nelisa.

"I think that tomorrow I should rescue my mother and sister too. I can't wait to see them. Moreover, it is also very easy because you already know where they are trapped."

"Nobody except Gismo and her soldiers know where your mother and sister are trapped. She knows how loyal we are to our queen and we can do anything for her. She has hidden them both in a secret place. It is not that easy Rosy.

Moreover, to rescue the Queen and the little princess you must confront Gismo. You don't know how powerful she is."

"OK," said Rosepink with disappointment.

She relaxed for the rest of the day, played with Timsi and practiced a bit of archery.

The Discovery Of Magic

Next day, Rosepink collected all her weapons and practiced for an hour before getting ready for the attack.

She went on her rescue mission, but when she reached the prison, she got to know that the key is with Gismo.

She could obviously not face Gismo directly. She touched the lock and said, “I wish this lock could open.” Magically, the lock opened.

Everyone was amazed.

Rosepink couldn’t believe it! She gazed at her hands in wonder.

“Am I dreaming? Is this true? Do I

actually have magical powers? If yes, then why didn't I know?" Rosepink was utterly confused.

"Yes, you have magical powers! Only you can defeat Gismo." A voice came out of her necklace for the first time.

Rosepink kept staring at her necklace until Nelisa interrupted, "Rosy, we are in Gismo's castle, not in our tunnel. We don't have much time."

"Nelisa, you don't know what I see in my necklace. I…I…I can see a lady and a small girl with her who looks so much like me when I was younger."

"Show me," said Nelisa and Arila in chorus. Rosepink showed them the necklace.

Their eyes were full of tears. "We are seeing our Queen after so many years," they said.

"What? My mom and sister!" Rosepink was astonished. She couldn't believe she was seeing her mother who was presumed dead and her little sister who did not even exist until a day ago.

"They were trying to show me the drawing of a ring. Yes, this one!" exclaimed Rosepink.

"I know this ring!" shouted Arila.

"Queen had magical powers and these powers were inherited. These were to be passed on from generation to generation. For that, you must do magic on your newborn child. Therefore, to make it easy, she transferred her powers in the form of a ring and a necklace. When you were born, she gave this necklace to you and kept the ring with her. As you know, Gismo snatched the ring from her. So now, she has no magical powers left with her. Only her legacy can use that ring."

"I wish I knew where they are," said Rosepink.

Her necklace indicated a glass chamber in which her mother and her sister were trapped. It was on top of a huge waterfall.

"I know this waterfall," said one of

the prisoners.

"Once we tried to run away and were caught near this waterfall. It is not a normal waterfall," he continued.

Water is very hot and whoever touches it is burnt right away. You will need to reach the top of that waterfall, carefully, without getting even a single burn. Then you can talk to her. One of us tried but couldn't balance for long and slipped."

"We have already walked halfway, right?" Rosepink asked Nelisa.

"Yes," replied Nelisa.

"So we three will go and meet mom. Others can go back," announced Rosepink.

"It's too dark, we can do that tomorrow also," said Nelisa.

"Please Nelisa," pleaded Rosepink.

"Please let her come. I can't wait to meet her," said the queen through the necklace.

"OK," agreed Nelisa.

"I think we should take Timsi too. Generally, she is of no good but maybe this time she comes handy," added Arila.

"You are right," agreed Nelisa.

Timsi gave them all a big smile.

The rescued prisoners went to the tunnel. One of the Prisoners guided Nelisa, Timsi, Arila and Rosepink to show them the way.

Can you climb
that up Timsi?

Rosy Meets Her Mother

When Rosepink went to climb up the mountain, Nelisa stopped her "Re-member Rosy, you are the only one, who can use the ring. We can't put your life at risk."

"Then who will go to meet my mother?"

"What about Timsi? She is also good at these things. Can you climb that up Timsi?" asked Arila

"I can for sure," said Timsi.

"I have an idea; I will shoot arrows in such a way that Timsi can use them as support, it would be easy and quick, suggested Rosepink."

They all agreed with the princess' idea.

Rosepink then shot arrows in a definite pattern. Timsi started climbing.

In the meantime, Rosepink was thinking about her mom. The woman in the glass chamber had long, entangled hair, as if she had not combed her hair for years. Her face was full of wrinkles and her eyes carried a tired look. She seemed very weak.

"I thought of a pretty young lady as my mother but this woman is so aged and old. Am I doing right by trusting these people? Are they using me? But this small girl in the glass chamber who came running towards that lady as if that lady is her mother, is mini me.

But that woman can't be my mother, she is so old, she seems to be 80 years old and surely my mother's age is not that much. Everything is so confusing here. What is the truth? How will I find that out?" Rosepink thought to herself.

"Oh Rosy, it is me only. I am your

mother. I am looking like that because I am trapped by Gismo and she gives me very little food. I provide the same to your sister. Therefore, I have grown very weak and aged early. Rosy! Gismo has cast such a spell on this waterfall that if anyone reaches the top of this waterfall, she will definitely slip and die," her mother spoke through the necklace.

Rosepink was still confused with so many unanswered questions running inside her head. She was also confused about the necklace speaking to her all of a sudden.

She thought that she had no other choice than to trust the maids. Everything was confusing but they did appear to be nice and honest people. She had no logical reason to doubt them but the confusion troubled her.

She kept her calm and tried to avoid negative thoughts.

All of a sudden, she realized what her mother had just said about the waterfall and noticed that Timsi was about to reach the top of falls.

"Stop Timsi!" she shouted at the top of her voice.

"Come back."

Then she told all of them what her Mom had just said.

Nelisa said, "Since you have the necklace, the spell won't affect you."

"That's true," assured Queen Lusida speaking through the necklace.

Then, Rosepink started climbing up the arrows. She was very happy to see her mom and sister.

"Mom!" she exclaimed.

Queen Lusida looked at Rosepink and they both kept looking at each other for a few moments. Both had tears in their eyes and froze for a few moments.

"Oh Rosy!" said Queen Lusida softly in a very low voice.

"Each and every moment that I have

spent here, I have been thinking about you and your father. Only the hope of meeting you both one day, has kept me alive. When Gismo trapped me here and told me, that she had killed Nelisa, Timsi and Arila, I was heart-broken. Giving birth to your sister gave a new meaning and purpose to my life."

While the queen was explaining Rosepink her struggles in the prison, the little girl ran towards her mother and hugged her tightly. "Mom, why are you crying?" she asked anxiously.

Queen Lusida hugged her back and said, "This is your elder sister, Princess Rosepink. She is the one, who will rescue us and take us back home. We will meet your father and everyone else. That is our world, my little princess – a beautiful world."

"I missed you so much mom!" Rospeink said looking at the little girl.

"What's the name of this cute little princess?"

"She doesn't have a formal name

yet. I call her 'Little'. I want you to give her a name," said her mom.

"So, I will name her…"

"Be quick!" interrupted Nelisa.

"Ok Nelisa," Rosepink shouted sadly.

"How can I rescue you mom?" Rosepink asked.

"For that, first you need the ring that I showed you and then when you have both, the necklace and the ring, rub them on this glass chamber and you can rescue us. After you rescue us, give me the ring and the necklace so that I can get my powers back. With the help of my powers, I can be back to my normal self and your sister too would become normal. After that you need to defeat Gismo," Rosepink's mother revealed the secret.

"I'll tell you how you will be able to do that. A black horse that she loves dearly is the source of all her powers. She does not leave that horse alone even for a moment.

If that horse is killed, Gismo will also die. As she is very aged and is alive only by using her powers, she has put her powers and life into that horse," the queen explained the story.

Rosy, a pink swan, created by magic, can only defeat that horse. This swan can be created only when the person wearing both the ring and the necklace recites a special spell. Rosy, only you can do that!" The queen told Rosepink.

"But where is the ring Mom?"

"Rosy, I feel Gismo is near us and she is coming this way."

"I will talk to you through the necklace and show you the place where the ring is hidden."

"I am glad that you came here and we can now use our magical powers through this necklace. Otherwise, you would have never known that it is magical. If I had this necklace with me, Gismo would have never been able to do anything. This necklace has all the defensive magical spells. She can't attack us at all in the presence of this necklace."

Rosepink smiled at her Mom and sister on hearing this and said, "We will go home soon Mom! Bye!"

"Bye!" Her sister smiled at her and her mother looked at them both with tears of joy.

On the other side, Gismo sensed that something wrong was happening in her castle. She had decided to visit Queen Lusida's chamber the next morning. "No, I should go right now," she thought.

Timsi In Trouble

Gismo then went to the waterfall. She saw that the queen and the little princess were sleeping.

Rosepink had rescued most of the prisoners by now. She could not sleep thinking of the future when her mother, sister and she would live happily in the kingdom. Next morning, Rosepink asked her mother through the necklace, "Mom, where is the ring?"

In her necklace, she could see a ring with a pink rose carved on it. It was hidden inside a pit under Gismo's bed. The pit was covered with a carpet.

"It's impossible to get that ring!" exclaimed Timsi.

"Why?" asked Rosepink

"Because at night, Gismo is in her room and in daytime, her soldiers guard her room."

"By the way who are her soldiers? I mean…"

"We know what you mean," interrupted Nelisa.

"The people she trapped earlier, now serve as her soldiers. She has hypnotized them by a spell and they have forgotten everything. They now think that they are the loyal and cruel soldiers of Gismo's army." "Ok. I should not harm them much. I just have to release them from the spell," said Rosepink.

"Yes," agreed Nelisa.

Arila entered the tunnel with some food and asked, "So what's today's plan?"

"I have an idea!" said Timsi.

"Seriously?" Nelisa asked mocking her.

"Yes!" she replied confidently.

Timsi shared the plan with everyone. They smiled at Timsi, appreciating her for the first time.

"I feel so proud that you liked my plan," said Timsi.

They spent the day making all the necessary preparations. The next day everyone got up very early and Rosepink practiced her moves for five hours.

According to the plan, Arila, Nelisa and Rosepink broke into the castle.

On the other hand, Timsi and the other rescued prisoners went to Gismo's garden, where she was busy eating fruits. They tried to keep Gismo busy so that Nelisa, Arila and Rosepink could carry out the plan of finding the ring.

"Gismo, the great, I have got these people for you," said Timsi greeting Gismo.

"Where did you find them?" asked

Gismo.

"I found them near my house, hiding in a tunnel."

"Who are you?"

"I am Timsi."

"Why have you come here?"

"To help you out."

Gismo gave a very weird look thinking that how could such a little girl help her.

"See, I think you have very less soldiers, as these prisoners were able to escape so easily."

"What do you mean?"

"I mean, I want to be your soldier. You can trust me. Look! I am not getting anything by living with these people. You are the God, Lord Gismo. You can provide me a good life if I serve you."

Everything was happening as per their plan.

Gismo was about to trust Timsi but Timsi made a huge mistake and said, "Lord Gismo you are so powerful! Everyone should pray to you and be your slave." Gismo smiled cunningly and captivated all the rescued prisoners along with Timsi in a magical prison.

"Oh! I think I overdid it again. I should have controlled my excitement," she said to herself.

"My first and foremost rule is not to trust anyone," said Gismo slyly as Timsi and her other friends looked at her sadly.

The Ring Is Nearby

Meanwhile Rosepink, Nelisa and Arila entered Gismo's castle, Nelisa said, "Let us please check if Timsi is alright. I am worried."

Rosepink asked her necklace about Timsi. The necklace showed her everything that had happened.

"Timsi!" Nelisa cried loudly.

"We shouldn't have involved her," she said weeping.

"Relax!" said Rosepink.

"Yes, Nelisa relax!" said Arila in a hoarse voice.

Suddenly there was a white flash and they could see nothing. They held each other's hands tightly.

Arila and Nelisa panicked. They thought everything was over and they all would all die a very painful death and started crying.

"How would we rescue everyone now?" Nelisa asked.

"Gismo has cast this spell so that if someone succeeds in entering the castle, the flash of light would make everything turn dark," said the voice from the necklace.

"Relax," said Rosepink calmly.

She did not panic and stayed focused.

"My father says," she said, "Where there is a will, there is a way. Till the time we have our mind to think, hands and feet to act, nobody can stop us."

"You guys can leave if you want but after reaching so close to the ring, I can't go back."

Nelisa and Arila thought about it and said, "Yes, we cannot go back. We are with you Rosy."

"Nelisa you have been to this place many times. We are in the hall right now, so where should we go?" Rosepink asked.

"We turn left from here," replied Nelisa.

They walked towards left. Suddenly they stumbled into something.

"I clearly remember there are five steps here," said Arila.

They climbed up the steps.

"Now where?"

"To the right, Rosy," said Nelisa.

They went to the right.

"There are three doors here. The one with the round knob is the door to Gismo's bedroom," told Arila.

They then felt the knob of each door.

The first one had a rectangular knob.

The second had a circular knob. To confirm, they checked the third knob. It was a triangular knob. They opened the second one.

"Oh, the ring is so near! I must be able to break the spell now," said her mother from the necklace. She tried but still couldn't do anything.

"I can't break the spell but I can feel the vibes of the ring. I can guide you. Keep walking straight, till I ask you to stop," said the necklace.

So, they all went straight. After about fifteen steps, Queen Lusida, through the necklace asked them to stop.

"I can feel the ring here. Take a few steps backwards." All of them stepped back.

"Can you feel something under your feet? Pull that shield which is coming between you and the ring."

Rosepink bent down and felt something like a carpet. Rosepink pulled it and there was a white flash again. Everything was visible now.

They saw Rosepink wearing the beautiful magical ring along with the necklace.

"At last it's time to go back home," chorused Nelisa and Arila.

"But how will we go to the waterfall?" Rosepink asked.

"You all will fly. You now have so many magical powers, Rosepink," said her mother from the necklace.

"Okay mom," said Rosepink.

They flew to the waterfall.

The Mystery Unfolds

Rosepink then rubbed the ring and the necklace on the glass chamber and rescued her mother and sister. She then gave the necklace and ring to her mother.

Queen Lusida wore the magical jewels and recited some magical words. Within seconds, the queen and her younger daughter turned young and beautiful. Their dresses changed to beautiful gowns and hair was neatly done.

"Oh Mom, you are so beautiful!" exclaimed Rosepink.

She looked at her younger sister

who now had red chubby cheeks with dark brown eyes and pretty, curly black hair.

"She is my little Chubby Cherry. I will always cherish this moment and call her princess *Cherry*," said Rosepink with tears of joy in her eyes.

"Oh!, Queen it's so good to see you released from the spell," said Nelisa.

"We have to be quick. Gismo will not sit quiet. Gismo and her horse are nowhere to be found," interrupted Arila.

"Yes, we must stop them from escaping, else they will return with more powers after five years to take revenge," remarked the queen.

Lusida then spoke some more magical words, but Arila interrupted, "Queen, Rosepink has to do this and catch them as per the plan."

"Sometimes, we have to adapt to the situation for good. I know, Rosepink can do that and I will be the happiest person to see her do that. But see, I don't want to take away this beautiful moment from her."

They all turned towards Rosepink. Both the princesses were smiling at each other. They hugged each other tightly as if they did not want to let the other one go.

They then held hands, walked towards the queen and hugged her tightly.

"We don't have much time left. The sun is about to set," the queen continued, "So let me use all my magical powers to pull them here."

She then carefully tied one end of the necklace to the ring, held it in her hands, and chanted some magical words.

Rosepink and Cherry listened carefully. In no time, Gismo and her horse were standing in front of them.

Gismo hurled spells at them angrily in a foreign language. Queen handed over the necklace and the ring to Rosepink.

She wore them quickly and turned into a beautiful shiny pink Swan.

Then within a fraction of second, before Gismo could even realize anything, the swan flew towards the horse and pecked on its head with her beak. Before Gismo could accept the situation, the horse began melting and dissolved in water.

There was huge blast and Rosepink turned back into the gorgeous princess. When the smoke settled, a pretty fairy, in a white dress appeared out of thin air, smiling at Rosepink and Queen Lusida. The fairy raised her magic wand, pointed it at Gismo, and killed her.

Then she turned towards Rosepink and Lusida and said, "Thank you Rosepink for releasing me from Gismo's spell. She had turned me into a horse and trapped me, as only I could kill her."

Saying so, the fairy disappeared.

"Nelisa, Arila look at you. You are no more dwarfs. You look so normal just like me and Mom!" said Rosepink.

Nelisa and Arila both looked at each other and smiled.

Then Timsi came with all the people who had been rescued from the pink rose.

They had all grown back to their original self. Everybody praised Rosepink.

The queen smiled and said, "Today is a big day. We all are free after six years of struggle. I am so proud of you, Rosepink- My Warrior Princess."

Everybody followed the queen and the two princesses.

Queen Lusida, Rosepink, Cherry, Nelisa and Arila climbed up the flight of stairs, and they were able to step out of the rose. Everyone else also came out of the flower.

Timsi called aloud from the staircase, and said excitedly "Rosy Posy you are just not listening to me! I have so much to tell you. Do you know, I executed the plans so perfectly, even then, Gismo understood that I was fooling her."

"Yes, my dear Timsi Vimsi," replied Rosepink with a big naughty smile.

"We all know that. You should be awarded with a new title, 'Miss Over Actor' of the Pink Rose."

Everybody laughed out loudly as they walked towards the palace.

Hi Friends,

Thank you for showing interest in my book. This is my first attempt at writing something like this and I look forward to your feedback on it. Share what you liked about this book and if you'd like to read more of similar stories. Your feedback is important to me. You can connect with me via the Facebook Page: **www.facebook.com/TheSecretPinkRose/**

-Niharika Chopra